T0132087

Santa's Reindeer Hay

By Fernan M. Gruber Jr.

ILLUSTRATIONS BY FLOYD YAMYAMIN

AuthorHouse™
1663 Liberty Drive
Bloomington, IN 47403
www.authorhouse.com
Phone: 1-800-839-8640

Published by AuthorHouse 06/14/2012

ISBN: 978-1-4685-9501-7 (sc)

Library of Congress Control Number: 2012907340

This book is printed on acid-free paper.

authorHOUSE®

This book is dedicated to :

Cody and Devon who inspired this story and my wife, Frieda who encouraged me to write it.

Supper and dessert are long past. The front door and living room windows are open. School is out, Spring is turning into Summer, and lilac blossoms scent the late evening air. A father, a carpenter by trade, sits studying a set of blue prints for a house he will build. A child lies upon a braided rug coloring a picture book laying on the hardwood floor before her.

The girl child is in thought about the other day and the white fuzzy haired and whisker faced gentleman whose eye blinked at her mother when he stood up after personally talking with her. It was the same kind of a twitch that she had seen mysteriously appear between her parents whenever they sometimes spoke of things that were sort-of over her head. She just had to talk to her all-knowing father about what she had seen.

"Daddy?" the girl said, stopping her coloring.

"Yes Splinter!" the father answered from behind his house plans.

"I think I saw Santa Clause." the child said, pushing up on her arms to eventually sit upright, her feet under her.

"When?" Her father asks, rolling up his blue prints.

"The other day and today." the girl answers.

"You did?: Her father's eyes widened.

"I knew who he was right-away . . . Mommy and I saw him at the Supermarket." squaring her shoulders, puffing up her chest, and in the deepest voice she could manage "He went "Ho! Ho! Ho!" . . ." and relaxes into her usual pretty-self, "Then he bent down, . . And asked me, "Have you been a good little girl?" . . . Only Santa would do that!""

The father leans forward laying his prints aside, and hums a questionable, "Hmm."

"Today! Mommy and I were on the way home and I saw him on a big green tractor . . . He waved at me, Daddy . . . His Santa Claus wave."

"He waved?" the father voiced in astonishment.

"Yes!" the little girl said, putting her hand up, slowly moving it back and forth, saying "Like this, Daddy."

"Well that seems like a Santa Clause wave alright . . ." and, in fatherly agreement and he asks, " . . . And what was he doing?"

"I . . . uh . . . think he was mowing some real tall grass, with a red machine pulled behind a dark green tractor."

"Hmm . . . could be!" the father agreed stroking his chin.

"But, wouldn't Santa be at the North Pole making toys?"

"Oh. . ! I don't know, Splinter? I hear he has a large staff of elves helping him make Christmas toys."

"But, why would he be cutting grass?"

"Well now, that is a good question? Lets see!.." The thought filled father rubbed his chin a moment. " . . . Maybe a disguise to check on children to see if they're minding their parents . . . . ."

The child interrupts, "Oh..! Daddy!"

" . . . . .or perhaps he's making hay for his reindeer?"

"Making hay? Why would Santa be doing that?

"Well living at the North Pole, as we all believe he does, he has to feed his reindeer just as farmers have to feed their animals in our country sides."

The girl's voice rising a bit as she questions her father, "He hasn't any reindeer hay. .At the North Pole?"

"No! I doubt it. The North Pole cold all year long covered in ice and snow . . . no! . .Santa may come down into our warmer climates to make the fodder he needs."

The girl questioningly giggles, "Fodder?"

"Fodder is what farm-folk sometimes call hay."

"Ah! Santa doesn't do that."

"What? . . Call the hay, fodder?"

"No, silly Daddy! . . Make hay!"

"What makes you so sure?" the father questions with a smile, looking his daughter straight in her eye.

"No! Nobody's ever seen him hauling any ol' hay away."

"Hmmm, . .I bet he does it at night," the father suggests.

"At night?" she asks, her eyes brightening more.

"Sure! That's why you never see him carrying the hay away." the father says.

With a quick come back, "He can't!"

"Why not?" her father asks.

"I'd hear him!" the little girl reasons.

The father reasons, "I doubt it . . ." as he moves a cupped hand near his ear, continuing " . . . Perhaps Mother Nature has provided the world with the crickets to drown out the sound of Santa's Summer sleigh-bells."

The girl shrugs her shoulders and says, "Santa can't use a sleigh in Summer."

"Why not?"

The girl snaps, "No snow!"

"You, my Splinter, are forgetting that Santa's sleigh is a magic sleigh, He doesn't need much snow nor room to land. He manages to land on roof-tops at Christmas time. And there isn't always snow everywhere he goes on Christmas-night."

The girl child frowning, "I never thought of that." Then came back with a change of thought and a glimmer in her voice, "Do you suppose we could put out some cookies and milk in a hay field for him?"

"Now why would you want to do that?" the father asks.

And, in a concerned look and toned voice she said, "Because he looked so awfully skinny."

Her father smilingly assures her, "I imagine Santa will look his fuller ol' self when he puts his warm Winter clothing on again come the next Christmas season."

Still holding a crayon, in her hand, looking as if she might be ready to rub her temple with it. "Daddy?"

"Yes Splinter!"

"If Santa Claus waits until night to move the reindeer hay, how does he find it in the dark?"

Her father hums once more, while looking towards the open door. "Hmm." . . . A glimmer of light entering his eyes, he says, "Perhaps Mother Nature's fireflies light the sides of the hay fields so Santa may know where to land."

"I never thought of that!"

There is a long silence between the father and daughter as he watches her grow.

The little girl changes the crayon in her hand for another to color the man's coveralls brown in her picture book.

Several minutes pass, and mother having noted the setting Sun and the time, stands in an open doorway saying, "Splinter, it is getting near bed time."

The girl hearing her mother, looking up says, "Daddy?"

"Yes Splinter." her father answers.

"Would it be alright if I sit by my window and listen to the crickets and watch the fireflies for a while?"

'Sure Splinter! . . .And, your mother and I'll be in, in a little while to tuck you in . . . right between the crickets and fireflies."

The little girl giggles saying, "Thank you Daddy." With a great big smile, she gets up, gives her mother and then her father a great big kiss, turns bending and picks-up her things and says as she leaves the room, "It's super. I can see Santa Claus anywhere, even in Summer. Even making reindeer hay. I wonder if I might just see him pass in the moon light tonight?"

Printed in the United States
by Baker & Taylor Publisher Services